T.R. Bear

T.R. IN NEW YORK

Terrance Dicks
Illustrated by Susan Hellard

Piccadilly Press · London

386067

JS.

T.R. Bear flew to New York
courtesy of Virgin Atlantic

Text Copyright © Terrance Dicks, 1989

Illustrations Copyright © Susan Hellard, 1989

Phototypeset by Area Graphics Ltd., Letchworth, Herts.
Printed and bound by MacLehose & Partners Ltd., Portsmouth
for the publishers, Piccadilly Press Ltd.,
5 Canfield Place, London NW6 3BT

British Library Cataloguing in Publication Data

Dicks, Terrance
T.R. in New York
I. Title   II. Hellard, Susan   III. Series
823′.914 [J]

ISBN 1-85340-050-5

Terrance Dicks. British. He lives in North London with his wife and sons.
He is the author of over one hundred books for children, including the
novelisations of Doctor Who, as well as being a television producer. His
series for Piccadilly Press include: *Sally Ann*, *The Adventures of Buster and
Betsy*, *The Adventures of David and Goliath*, *A Cat called Max* and
Jonathan's Ghost.

Susan Hellard. British. She lives in North London, and is a young illustrator
with a growing international reputation, well known for her wry sense of
humour. She has illustrated a number of titles for Piccadilly Press including
the *Dilly the Dinosaur* series, the *Lift-the-Flap* picture books and a number
of other picture books.

Chapter One

The Boy Who Knew Too Much

'Message for Mr Bear! Message for Mr Bear!'

The uniformed messenger-boy wandered through the crowded lobby of the luxurious Gotham Hotel on New York's Fifth Avenue. Sitting in a big leather armchair in a quiet corner, Jimmy looked at the teddy bear in the open school-bag beside him. 'Maybe it's for you, T.R.!'

1

Jimmy was so amazed to find himself actually in New York that almost anything seemed possible. His father was a history lecturer who had written a series of best-selling history books for children. He'd been asked to speak at a big History Conference in New York. Jimmy's mother was giving an exhibition of her pottery, and his brother and sister were tied-up with exams, so Jimmy had been the only one able to go with him. Jimmy and, of course, T.R. Bear.

Short and stocky, bespectacled and tough, T.R. was an All-American teddy bear named after his hero, the long-ago president Theodore Roosevelt. When he wanted to, he could come to life.

The messenger-boy was

moving in their direction.
'Message for Mr Bear! Message
for Mr Bear . . .' To Jimmy's
horror, T.R. boomed, 'Over
here, boy!' and the page-boy
came hurrying towards them.

He looked round for the owner
of the deep booming voice.
'Message for Mr Bear?'

'Er . . . he was called to the telephone,' stammered Jimmy. Actually it was Jimmy's dad who'd been called to the phone.

The messenger-boy put a white envelope on the table. 'Well, this is for him. Do me a favour and see he gets it.' The messenger hurried away. Like everyone else in New York, he seemed to be in a great rush.

Jimmy looked at T.R. 'Now see what you've done!'

T.R. did his best to look innocent. 'Who me? A guy

bellows out my name so naturally I answer . . .'

'Well, you're not supposed to, are you, not in public . . .'

'You accepted the message, kid.'

'Yes, I did, didn't I? I just sort of panicked.' Jimmy looked at the envelope. 'Well, it isn't for you, anyway! Look, the name's spelt B-a-y-e-r.' The envelope was

unsealed, and he couldn't resist looking inside. But there was nothing to look at – the envelope was empty.

Jimmy slipped the envelope into his pocket, grabbed his school-bag, and stood up. 'I'd better go and sort things out – they must have forgotten to put the message in the envelope.'

The Gotham Towers was a very posh hotel indeed – luckily the Conference people were paying the bill. The hotel had a huge marble-floored lobby with a fountain playing in the centre, and the Reception Desk was right on the other side. Across the lobby, Jimmy saw two strange, sinister-looking men staring hard at him. One was big and fat, the

other thin and weaselly. As he
walked across the lobby, they
started to move towards him.
When they met in the middle the
two men closed in on him,
blocking his way to the desk.

'My dear little fellow,' said the
fat man in a rich, fruity voice.
'What a very great pleasure it is to
see you again. And where is our

mutual friend, Mr Bayer?'

'I'm afraid there's been a mistake,' began Jimmy.

The weaselly man had slipped round behind him. 'There most certainly has,' he hissed, 'and you have made it. Now, where is Bayer? Tell us, or it will be the worse for you!'

Jimmy felt what was obviously a pistol-barrel poking into the small of his back. 'You will come

with us, quietly please,' hissed the weaselly man.

Jimmy didn't move. 'Listen, whoever you are, this is all a silly mistake. I'm not the one you want.'

'Indeed?' purred the fat man. 'Then tell me this – why did you claim the message for Mr Bayer?'

'It was just a joke . . .'

He felt another jab in the ribs.

'So? We enjoy a joke,' said the weaselly man. 'You will come with us, and we shall all have a good laugh.'

'If you'd only listen . . .'

'I am losing patience,' said the fat man. 'Will you come on your feet, or shall we be obliged to knock you out and carry you?'

Jimmy started walking towards

the main door. Just as they reached the door, the fat man paused. 'The bag! Better check the bag!'

The little man rummaged inside the bag, and produced T.R. 'There is only this stupid toy.'

He was about to stuff the little bear back when the fat man said, 'Don't be so hasty. In our business, things are seldom what they seem. That little bear could conceal many things, a recording machine, a tracking device, even a bomb!'

To Jimmy's horror the little man produced an enormous knife. 'Shall I investigate?'

The fat man chuckled. 'Even in New York, the public

dismembering of a teddy bear
might cause some comment. No,
just leave the creature here, then
it can do us no harm.'

The weaselly man tossed T.R.
carelessly onto the nearest chair.

'Now,' said the fat man, 'our
carriage awaits. This way, my
dear young friend!'

The two men bustled Jimmy
out of the door on to busy Fifth

Avenue. Jimmy was hustled into a big black limousine that was waiting at the kerb. Immediately, the limousine swept away.

Jimmy sat on the luxuriously padded back seat, wedged between the thin man and the fat man, scarcely able to believe what had happened to him. His first day in New York and he'd been kidnapped!

Chapter Two

'The Name's Bear –
James Bear!'

Left alone in his chair, T.R.
came instantly to life. Not caring
if he was seen or not, he jumped
down from the chair and shot out
through the open front door, just
in time to see the big black
limousine pull away.

A battered yellow taxi cab
drew up outside the hotel and as
the passenger, a large lady in an
expensive fur coat, got out, T.R.

jumped in, unseen by the large lady, and by the hotel doorman who opened and closed the taxi door.

The second the cab had been paid off, T.R. growled, 'Okay driver, follow that black limo!'

The driver was a typical New York cabbie, tough and cynical. 'And who are you, Buster?' he growled. He glanced over his shoulder. 'Come to that, *where* are you?'

'I'm crouching down so the guys in the limo don't see my face.'

The driver wasn't happy. 'I think you'd better get out of my cab before I call a cop.'

T.R. used his toughest voice. 'Listen, dummy, do you know

who I am? Special Agent T.R.
Bear. Now, will you get moving,
or do I book you for obstructing
the U.S. Government?'

'On my way, Mr Bear!' With a
grinding of gears, the taxi pulled
out into the traffic, following the
black limousine.

*   *   *

Jimmy was sitting on a hard wooden chair in the middle of an abandoned warehouse, blinking in the light of the one powerful lamp hanging from a wire just over his head. Standing over him, just outside the little circle of light, were his two captors, the little thin man and the big fat one. They were taking it in turn to fire questions at him.

'Where is Bayer?'

'How long have you been working with him?'

'What does he look like?'

'*Where is Bayer now*?'

But all Jimmy could say in reply was, 'I don't know. I just don't know . . .'

Finally the fat man said, 'I'm afraid we're wasting our time. Our young friend is obstinate.'

'Leave him to me,' snarled the weaselly man. 'I will make him talk.'

As the thin man advanced towards him, raising his hand, Jimmy cowered back in the chair. 'All right, all right, I'll tell you . . .'

'I thought so,' snarled the thin man. 'Well, go on, boy. Talk!'

Jimmy had no intention of telling the real truth – they'd never believe him. Instead he decided to make up a story they *would* believe. 'I was sitting in the lobby when this man came up to me. He said he was expecting an important message but he had to leave the hotel and didn't want to miss it. He said if I'd listen out for a message for a Mr Bayer and collect it when it came and keep it for him, he'd make it worth my while.' Jimmy shrugged. 'There didn't seem any harm in it, so I agreed.'

There was a moment's pause. Then the thin man shouted, 'You're lying!' He advanced on Jimmy again.

'Wait,' said the fat man silkily. 'Suppose the boy is telling the truth.'

'But why would Bayer do such a thing?'

The fat man became very angry. 'You fool, isn't that obvious?'

'Not to me, no,' said the thin man sulkily.

'My dear fellow, we wait to see who collects the message. But

Bayer knows that we are after him. He sets up a decoy, and simply waits to see who collects his collector! Instead of our identifying him, he identifies us. One has to admire the fellow!'

The thin man gave a gasp of horror. 'You mean – Bayer was watching us all the time? He could have followed us here!'

A voice boomed out from the darkness beyond the lamplight.

'Congratulations, fatso, you worked it all out – just a little too late!'

Both men whirled round, their hands going to their pockets. 'Who is that?' quavered the fat man.

'The name's Bear – James Bear – and I've got you covered. So get those hands in the air!'

Jimmy just couldn't believe his ears. Somehow or other, T.R. had come to his rescue.

Chapter Three
The Missing Microfilm

Slowly the two men raised their hands.

The fat man said, 'Congratulations, Mr Bayer, you've outsmarted us. You're a character, sir, you really are! Now then, surely we can make a deal?'

'What kind of a deal?'

'You want to find that missing microfilm and so do we. Help us to find the French lady and make her reveal its whereabouts, and we'll share the profits, fifty-fifty.'

'What do you know about the French lady?'

'Only what our poor friend Otto was able to tell us before he, er – passed on. Soon after he stole the microfilm he was most unfortunately shot.'

'Yes, and I bet I know who shot him,' thought Jimmy.

Smoothly the fat man went on, 'Unfortunately he was rambling towards the end. With his dying gasp he said, "If you want the microfilm you'll have to visit Frenchy . . . The French lady's got it all in her head." Now sir, we believe you know how to find this Frenchy.'

'Maybe I do and maybe I don't,' said the voice.

'A Government secret agent isn't too well paid – and I offer riches. Do we have a deal?'

'I'll think about it. Now, you two stay just where you are! Come on, kid!'

Jimmy jumped out of the chair and ran towards the voice. As he'd expected, T.R. Bear was waiting in the shadows. 'How did you get here?'

'By taxi – and he's still waiting, with the meter running. This way!'

T.R. led him towards a little square of light in the distance. They ran through the door and across the warehouse yard to the run-down street, where a battered yellow taxi was waiting just a little way ahead. Grabbing T.R. and shoving him in the bag, Jimmy ran up behind the taxi and jumped in the back seat. 'Hotel Gotham, Fifth Avenue please – and hurry!'

'Sorry, kid, this taxi's reserved for Mr Bear.'

Before the driver could turn round T.R. growled, 'Don't worry, I'm here too. Now, you heard the kid, Hotel Gotham – and step on it!'

Suddenly a bullet whined over the cab. Looking out of the window, Jimmy saw the two men who'd kidnapped him running out of the warehouse with guns in their hands.

Starting the engine, the driver

put his foot down, and the taxi roared away . . .

*   *   *

When they reached the Hotel Gotham, Jimmy paid the driver and added a generous tip. It took a big chunk out of his holiday spending money, but he reckoned it was worth it.

The driver looked round puzzled. 'What happened to the special agent guy, Mr Bear?'

'Oh, he slipped out at a red light,' said Jimmy hurriedly. 'He likes to keep out of sight as much as he can.'

'He sure does,' said the driver. 'All the time I've been working on this job with him and I ain't never set eyes on him.' With a friendly wave the driver zoomed

away, and Jimmy went back
through the big doors into the
lobby of the Hotel Gotham.

He found his father sitting in an
armchair, studying a map of New
York. 'Ah, there you are. Been
for a walk? You might have left
me a message, I was getting a bit
worried.'

'Sorry, Dad,' said Jimmy. 'You

might say I got carried away.'

'Well, come on, let's get on with it!'

'On with what?' asked Jimmy.

'The sightseeing, of course.

I've only got today, after that I'll be tied up with the Conference. I've got it all worked out . . .'

Outside the hotel, his father stood on the pavement for a moment, checking the map. 'We'll start with the Empire State Building, right here on Fifth Avenue. This way!'

As Jimmy's father marched ahead, Jimmy heard T.R. whisper, 'Look behind you, kid.'

Jimmy glanced over his shoulder, and saw a big black limousine draw up at the kerb.

The thin man and the fat man jumped out. Jimmy hurried off after his father – and the two men followed.

'What are they up to, T.R.?' whispered Jimmy. 'Will they

try and kidnap me again?'

T.R. shook his head. 'I doubt it. They're going to stick with you till you meet up with this French dame they talked about.'

'But we're not going to meet her,' said Jimmy.

'You know that and I know that,' said T.R. 'But do those two guys know it? I reckon they plan to tag along till they catch you and the French lady together – then they'll close in for the kill!'

Chapter Four

The Bear Who Came in from the Cold

As the morning went on it looked as if T.R.'s theory was right.

The two sinister men stayed right behind them.

They followed them to the viewing gallery on the hundred-and-second storey of the Empire State Building with its amazing fifty-mile view all round Manhattan.

'Actually the World Trade Centre's the tallest building now,' said Jimmy's father, nose buried in his guide book. 'But the Empire State always used to be.

It's the one King Kong climbed in the original black-and-white movie.'

They moved on to the Rockefeller Centre, toured the

famous Radio City Music Hall
and watched the skaters whirling
round on the huge ice rink.

Jimmy could almost feel the
eyes of the two men boring into
his back and, sure enough, when
he turned round, there they were.

When they ate lunch –
hamburger, chips and coke, in a
nearby restaurant – two sinister
figures were at the next table.

They were still there at the

huge Museum of Modern Art, trailing him through the different galleries . . . Then somewhere between the Egyptian Galleries and the American Wing, they seemed to disappear.

'Maybe they've got lost,' whispered Jimmy hopefully. They were sitting in the glassed-in garden in the American Wing, and his father was studying the guide book.

T.R. looked doubtful, but
before he could reply, Jimmy's
father said, 'Well, I reckon we've
got time for just one more visit –
what's it to be?' He passed over
the guide book. 'Here, you
decide while I have a quick look
round the garden . . .'

Jimmy flicked through, and
found there was only one obvious
choice. He started reading about
it in more detail . . . and gave a
sudden gasp of astonishment.
'T.R. I've got it!'

'Got what, kid?'

'Everything,' said Jimmy, his
voice rising in excitement. 'I
know who the French lady is and
where she is – I even know where
Otto hid the missing microfilm!'

'Well, I'd keep quiet about it if

I were you,' growled T.R. But it was already too late.

The bushes behind him parted and a weaselly face appeared, staring at them over a gun-barrel. 'You will give me this information.'

'Oh no I won't,' said Jimmy and shoved hard; the thin man tumbled backwards into the greenery.

Jumping up, he slung the bag with T.R. in over his shoulder and dashed for the exit, grabbing his dad by the hand on the way. 'Come on, Dad, I know exactly where I want to go, but if we don't get a move on it'll be closed for the day.'

He rushed his father along the corridors at top speed, ignoring the shouts from behind them.

As they reached the main entrance, Jimmy heard a fruity voice ring out. 'Those two, the man and the boy with the bag – stop them! I've just seen them steal a valuable painting. It's in the boy's bag . . .'

'What's all that about?' asked Jimmy's father. 'He doesn't mean us, does he?'

'No, of course not,' said Jimmy, hauling him out of the door. A taxi was passing by, and Jimmy waved it down and shoved his father inside. 'Statue of

Liberty, please – and hurry!'

As the cab set off, Jimmy glanced out of the window and saw the fat man and the thin man dash out of the Museum with some kind of security guard. The security man flagged down a passing police car and pointed to their taxi. To Jimmy's horror, the police car set off after them. Jimmy just had time to see the two men's black limousine draw up, then the cab turned a corner . . .

The evening rush-hour traffic was just beginning, and the yellow cab wove through it with practised speed, blasting its horn at anyone who got in the way. All the time they heard the howl of the police siren behind them.

The taxi driver laughed. 'You might almost think those guys were after us.'

'Yes, you might,' said Jimmy. 'Do you think you can get us to the Statue before it closes?'

'Well, I can get you to the ferry terminal. You have to get the boat out to Liberty Island. Long as you get the last ferry, you'll be okay . . .'

'Please try,' said Jimmy. 'We've only got today, so if I don't see the Statue tonight, I won't see it at all.'

'Hey, we can't have that now,' said the driver, and put his foot down.

They made the last ferry to the island with minutes to spare, and as the little boat pulled away,

Jimmy saw first a police car and then a big black limousine draw up.

He gave a sigh of relief, and found a quiet corner of the deck, so he could talk to T.R. 'It's all right now. This is the last boat, so we'll be able to get to the Statue before any of them.'

'How about some explanations?' growled T.R. 'How come you had this blinding flash of inspiration?'

'It's all in the guide book,' explained Jimmy. 'The Statue of Liberty was presented to America by the French people. She was made in France. She's a French lady!' He pointed to the towering shape of the enormous statue with its torch held high, now growing steadily nearer. 'And there she is!'

They got off the ferry and followed the other tourists, only a handful of them this late in the day, through a kind of park to the building in the base of the Statue. They rode up in a lift to the viewing gallery near the top, and stood looking at the amazing view.

But Jimmy didn't seem to be satisfied. He found an attendant. 'Can we get any higher?'

'There's a smaller viewing chamber actually in the Statue's head . . . It's a heck of a climb, though.'

Jimmy's dad was absorbed in the view and didn't notice when they moved away. Jimmy looked

at T.R. 'It's all in the French lady's head,' said Jimmy. 'Come on!'

They set off up an incredibly steep spiral staircase.

Luckily everybody else had been put off by the climb, and the little room was empty.

T.R. jumped out of the bag and they began to search. The room was quite small and bare, and there just weren't all that many places to look.

'I give up,' said Jimmy at last.

'Never do that,' said T.R. He pointed to a little magnetic box stuck to the base of a metal pillar.

'Well done,' said Jimmy. Pocketing the box and putting T.R. back in the bag, he began the steep climb down to the main gallery.

When they reached it, there were only three people in the viewing gallery. Jimmy's dad, a fat man and a thin man. The thin man was holding a gun.

Jimmy's dad was looking totally confused. 'Everybody else went down, and these two came up,' he explained. 'They've been babbling about microfilm or something, can't make head or tail of it.'

'I think you understand very well what we want,' said the fat man smoothly. 'The microfilm is now in our young friend's possession. I realised the truth as soon as you made your dash for the Statue. All in the French lady's head, eh? Most amusing!'

The thin man, as usual, was deadly serious. 'So, you will now hand it over – or else . . .'
He raised his revolver.

Jimmy heard a low growl from the bag. 'Okay, kid, pitch me at him. Do it!'

Grabbing T.R., Jimmy threw him at the thin man. T.R. zoomed through the air as if fired

from a cannon, and hit the thin
man's gun. It flew through the
air, and Jimmy's dad, who'd been
quite a decent cricketer when
younger, fielded it automatically.
The fat man and the thin man put
their hands up.

The lift doors sighed open
revealing a stocky man in trench-
coat, dark glasses and hat. 'I see

I needn't have worried,' he said admiringly. Behind him were lots of burly New York policemen who grabbed the fat man and the thin man with brisk efficiency, and took them away in the lift.

When they'd all gone there was only the stocky man left.

He showed Jimmy's father a badge in a leather folder. 'Jim Bayer, sir. U.S. Government agent. I've been following you, acting as your back-up all the time. I'm sorry those two characters even got to you, they hi-jacked a boat and we had to wait for the police launch. Oh, and we cleared up all that nonsense at the Museum. I had to drop a hint about who you were.'

'Oh, that's all right,' said Jimmy's father, who clearly didn't

have the slightest idea what was going on.

'And now if you don't mind, sir,' said the agent politely.

Jimmy's dad looked baffled. 'Sorry? Oh, this.' He handed over the thin man's gun.

'This is what he wants,' said Jimmy, and passed his father the little metal box. His father handed it over.

Bayer opened it and sighed with relief. 'I'm very grateful for all your help, sir. I knew we'd asked the British Secret Service to help find the microfilm, but I didn't expect you so soon. Those two guys were on to me at the hotel so I had to lay low.' He shook his head admiringly. 'Boy, the smooth way you two moved in and took over . . . You flushed them out, they kept tabs on you, and I kept tabs on them. It was just a great honour to work with you, sir.' Touching his hat in salute, he went down in the lift.

Jimmy's father scratched his head. 'Nice chap that, but a bit confused. He seems to have got me mixed up with someone else.'

Jimmy grinned. 'I'd make the

most of it if I were you, Dad. It's not every day you get taken for James Bond . . .'

But on the ferry-boat back from Liberty Island Jimmy hugged T.R. and whispered, 'I'm sorry we had to let Dad take all the credit, but we know who's the real hero, don't we? Special Agent T.R. Bear!'